The Glitter Bug

Read more
UNICORN DIARIES
books!

1. Unicorn Diaries: Bo's Magical New Friend — Rebecca Elliott
2. Unicorn Diaries: Bo and the Dragon-Pup — Rebecca Elliott
3. Unicorn Diaries: Bo the Brave — Rebecca Elliott
4. Unicorn Diaries: The Goblin Princess — Rebecca Elliott

5. Unicorn Diaries: Bo and the Merbaby — Rebecca Elliott
6. Unicorn Diaries: Storm on Snowbelle Mountain — Rebecca Elliott
7. Unicorn Diaries: The Missing Magic — Rebecca Elliott
8. Unicorn Diaries: Welcome to Sparklegrove — Rebecca Elliott

9. Unicorn Diaries: The Glitter Bug — Rebecca Elliott
10. Unicorn Diaries: Bo and the Witch — Rebecca Elliott

Unicorn Diaries

The Glitter Bug

Rebecca Elliott

BRANCHES

SCHOLASTIC INC.

For Sam and Kevin. XX —R.E.

Special thanks to Clare Wilson
for her contributions to this book.

Copyright © 2023 by Rebecca Elliott

All rights reserved. Published by Scholastic Inc., *Publishers since 1920.*
SCHOLASTIC, BRANCHES, and associated logos are trademarks
and/or registered trademarks of Scholastic Inc.

The publisher does not have any control over and does not assume
any responsibility for author or third-party websites or their content.

No part of this publication may be reproduced, stored in a retrieval system,
or transmitted in any form or by any means, electronic, mechanical,
photocopying, recording, or otherwise, without written permission of the
publisher. For information regarding permission, write to Scholastic Inc.,
Attention: Permissions Department, 557 Broadway, New York, NY 10012.

This book is a work of fiction. Names, characters, places, and incidents are
either the product of the author's imagination or are used fictitiously, and any
resemblance to actual persons, living or dead, business establishments,
events, or locales is entirely coincidental.

Library of Congress Cataloging-in-Publication Data

Names: Elliott, Rebecca, author, illustrator.
Title: The glitter bug / Rebecca Elliott.
Description: First edition. | New York : Branches/Scholastic
Inc., 2023. | Series: Unicorn diaries; 9 | Audience: Ages 5–7. |
Audience: Grades K–2. | Summary: Bo Tinseltail and friends meet a
kitsune who helps them find a cure after they all catch the Glitter Bug.
Identifiers: LCCN 2022038511 (print) | ISBN
9781338880366 (paperback) | ISBN 9781338880403 (library binding)
Subjects: CYAC: Unicorns–Fiction. | Mythical animals–Fiction. |
Diseases–Fiction. | Friendship–Fiction. | Diaries–Fiction. | BISAC:
JUVENILE FICTION / Readers / Chapter Books | JUVENILE FICTION / Animals
/ Dragons, Unicorns & Mythical | LCGFT: Diary fiction.
Classification: LCC PZ7.E45812 Gl 2023 (print) | DDC [Fic]–dc23
LC record available at https://lccn.loc.gov/2022038511

ISBN 978-1-338-88040-3 (hardcover) / ISBN 978-1-338-88036-6 (paperback)

10 9 8 7 6 5 4 3 2 1   23 24 25 26 27

Printed in China   62
First edition, October 2023

Edited by Katie Carella and Cindy Kim
Book design by Marissa Asuncion

Table of Contents

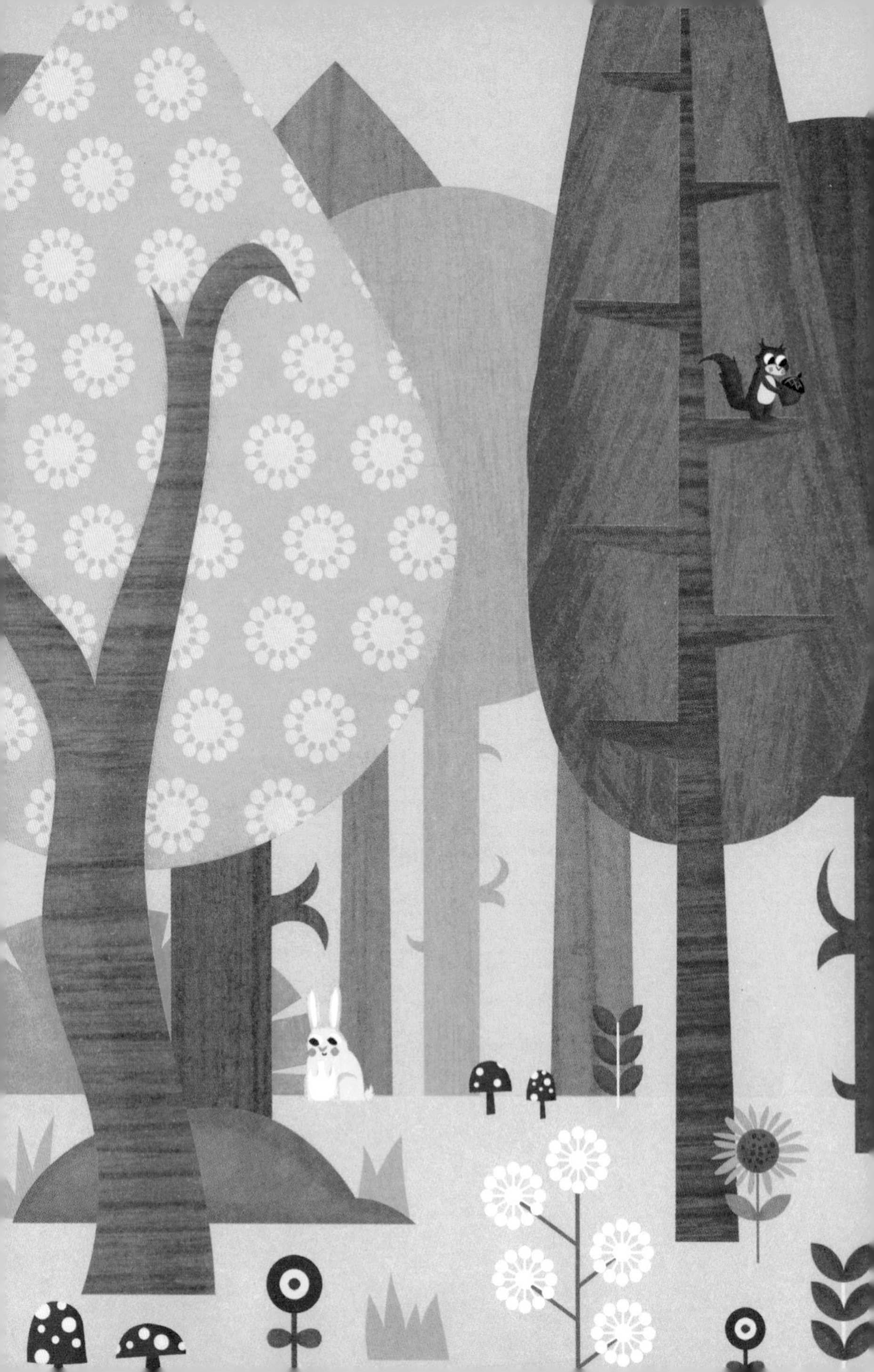

1

Hello – ACHOO!

Sunday

ACHOO!

Excuse me, Diary! I don't know why, but I keep sneezing. Anyway, hello! It's me, Bo, short for Rainbow – **ACHOO!** Tinseltail. (Oops! Achoo isn't my middle name!)

Did you know unicorns sneeze glitter? Let me tell you some other glittery-good things about us while I tidy up.

Rainbow Falls

Gnome Tunnels

Troll Caves

Glimmer Glade

Sparklegrove School for Unicorns

Dragon Nests

Budbloom Meadow

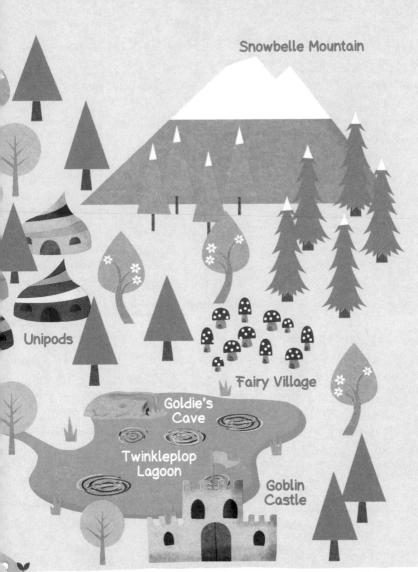

Snowbelle Mountain

Unipods

Fairy Village

Goldie's Cave

Twinkleplop Lagoon

Goblin Castle

Lots of magical creatures live here and others visit. Like kitsunes!

Here's what I know about kitsunes:

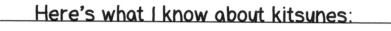

You say their name like this: KEE-TSOO-NAYs.

They look like foxes but have lots of tails!

They earn up to nine tails for doing kind and clever things.

They heal creatures in exchange for gold.

Now back to unicorns. Here are more facts about us:

Horn
Useful for planting flowers in the ground.

Eyes
When we look at stars, our eyes twinkle.

Nose
Sneezing makes a LOT of glitter!

Mouth
When we snore, it sounds like music.

Want to learn more unicorn facts?

Our horns glow when we're nervous. They also glow when it's dark or when we want to read!

We live in **UNIPODS**.

We only eat very colorful food.

Golden Glow

Purple
Cupkins

Cake

Rainbow
Super Soup

Lucky Lollipops

Our favorite things are laughter, friendship, and rainbows.

HA!

HA!

My friends and I go to Sparklegrove School for Unicorns (S.S.U.). Our teacher is Mr. Rumptwinkle. He's a Shape-Shifter Unicorn, so sometimes he's difficult to spot!

All unicorns have different unicorn powers. I'm a Wish Unicorn, so I can grant one wish every week.

Here are all my fellow S.S.U. pals and their magical powers.

Nutmeg Silvertips
Flying Unicorn

Scarlett Sugarlumps
Thingamabob Unicorn

Jed Glitterock
Weather Unicorn

Monty Dumpling
Size-Changer Unicorn

Piper Forestine
Healer Unicorn

Sunny Huckleberry
Crystal-Clear Unicorn

At school, we learn **GLITTERRIFIC** stuff like:

RAINBOW DANCING

BUBBLE-POP
(Our favorite sport.)

SNOW JUMPING

CRYSTOLOGY
(Crystals are super powerful!)

★ 10 ★

We learn something new every week. When we succeed, Mr. Rumptwinkle gives us each a special unicorn patch. I love adding patches to my blanket.

ACHOO! Well, if we're earning a sneeze patch this week, I think I already deserve it!

Good night, Diary!

2

The Glitter Bug

When I woke up today, I was still sneezing. There was glitter all over my cloud bed! I started to worry something could be wrong, so I spoke to my BFF Sunny.

Sunny, I keep —

ACHOO!

Sneezing?

YES! Unicorns don't get sick often, so this is strange.

Don't worry, Bo. We can figure it out.

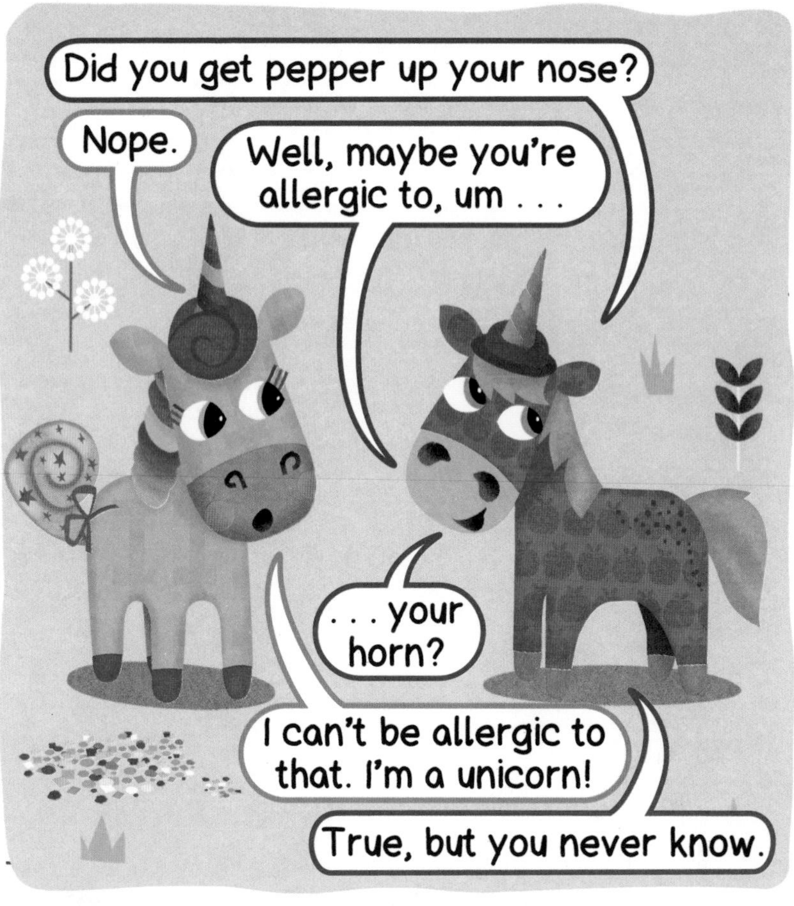
Did you get pepper up your nose?
Nope.
Well, maybe you're allergic to, um . . .
. . . your horn?
I can't be allergic to that. I'm a unicorn!
True, but you never know.

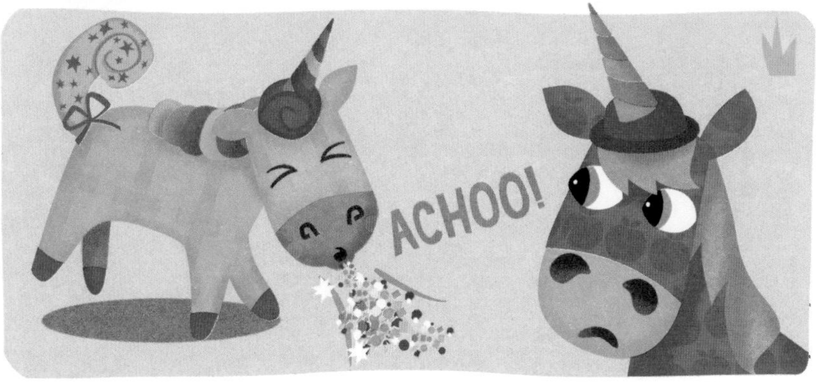
ACHOO!

We decided to see if the other unicorns might know what was wrong.

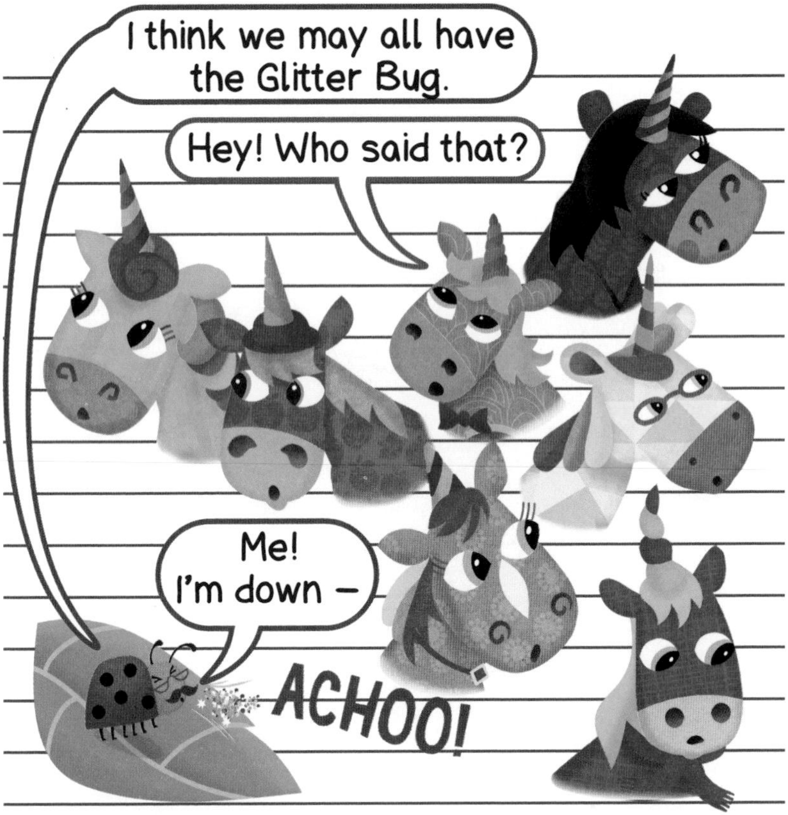
I think we may all have the Glitter Bug.
Hey! Who said that?
Me! I'm down –
ACHOO!

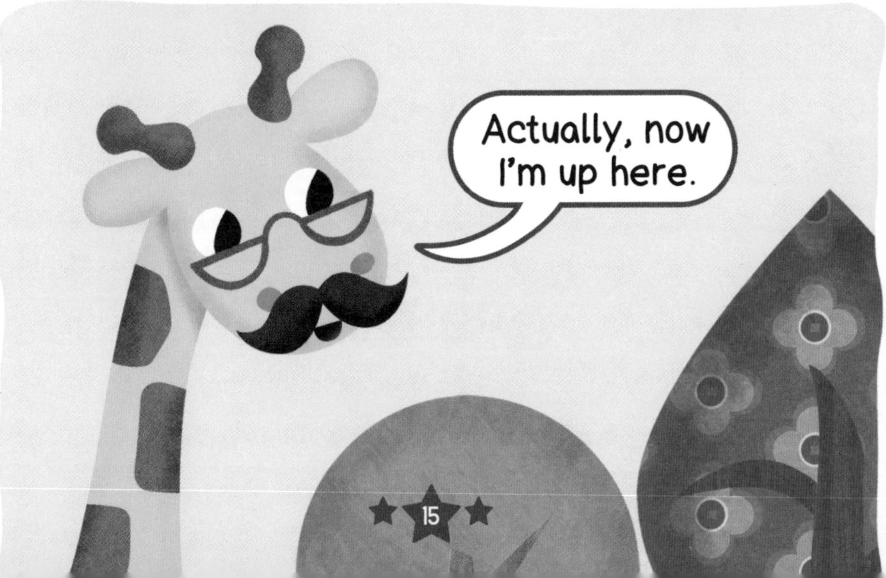
Actually, now I'm up here.

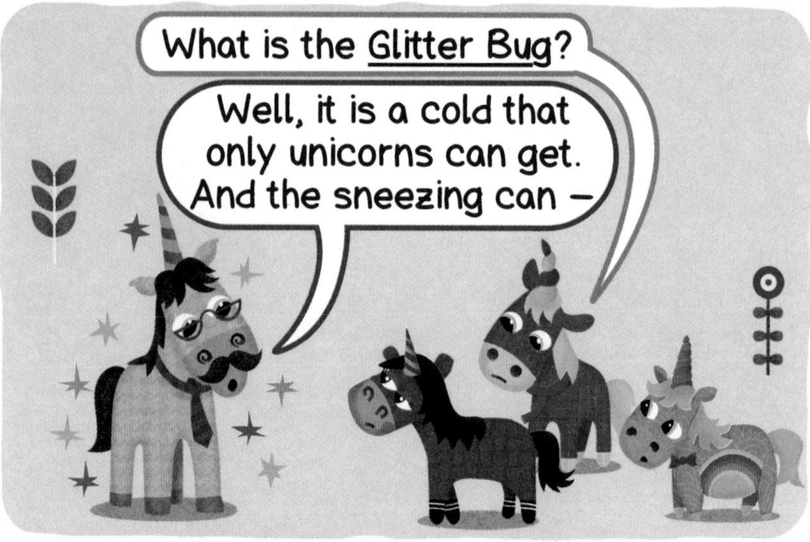
What is the Glitter Bug?
Well, it is a cold that only unicorns can get. And the sneezing can –

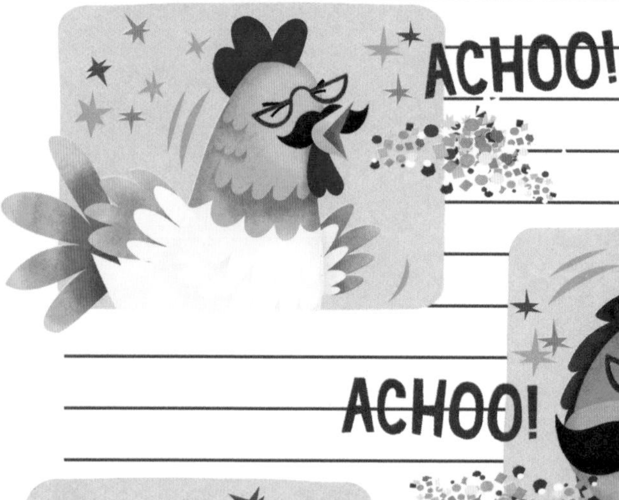
ACHOO!

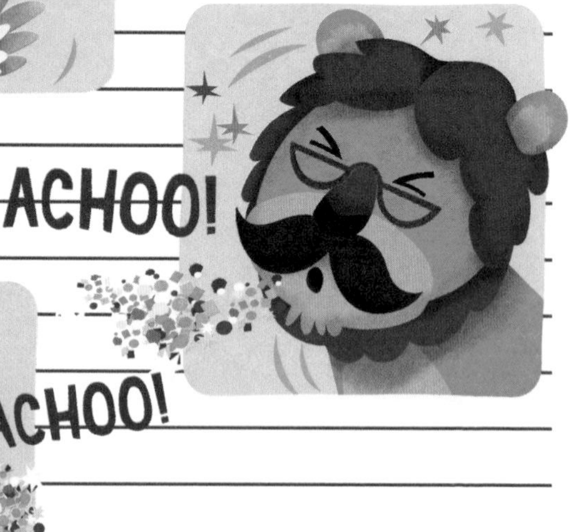
ACHOO!

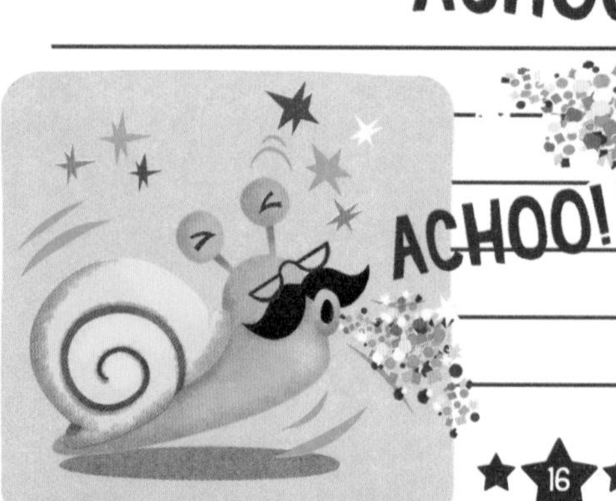
ACHOO!

Just then, Scarlett did a big sneeze, and a confused parrot appeared from her mane!

ACHOO!

Okay. Maybe I spoke too soon!

★ 17 ★

We all kept sneezing, and it was tiring us out!

Piper tried to make her healing powers work.

But nothing happened!

I tried to make Sunny's wish come true, but nothing happened!

So, after tidying up lots of glitter, we went to bed early. Oh, Diary, I hope we feel better tomorrow!

3

Sneezy Does It

At breakfast, we were all still sneezing. Poor Scarlett kept magicking up stuff from her mane, and Mr. Rumptwinkle kept shapeshifting.

Mr. Rumptwinkle and Scarlett seem really sick.

Yeah. Their sneezes keep setting off their powers.

Well, I'm glad you're not as sick as we are.

Then we ALL sneezed at the same time and —

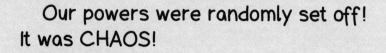

Our powers were randomly set off!
It was CHAOS!

ACHOO!

ACHOO!

ACHOO!

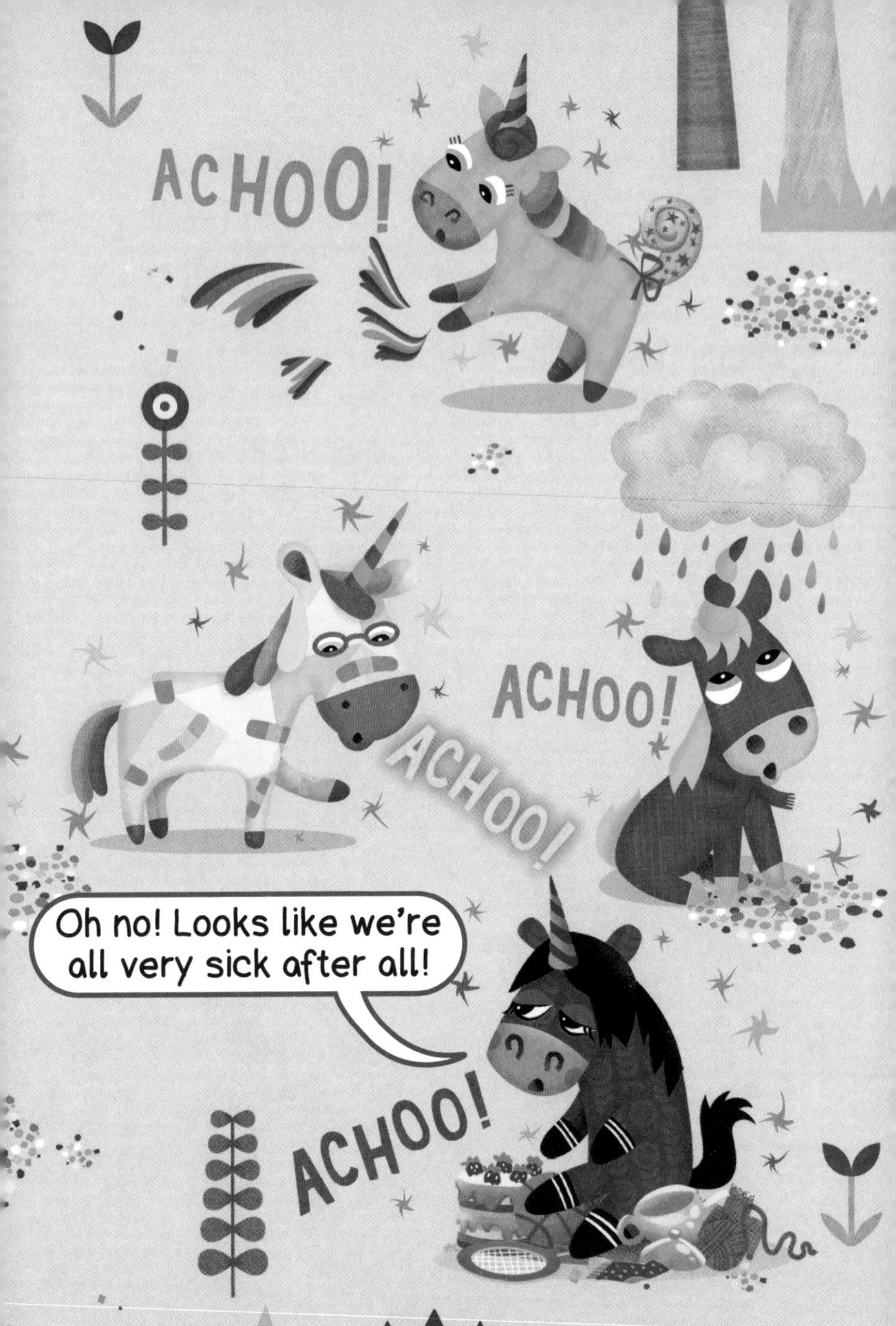

ACHOO!
ACHOO!
ACHOO!
Oh no! Looks like we're all very sick after all!
ACHOO!

After we tidied up all the glitter,
Mr. Rumptwinkle had some bad news.

Unicorns, I'm sorry. I think you're all too sick to earn a patch this week. We need to focus on helping one another get better.

But what if we never stop sneezing?!

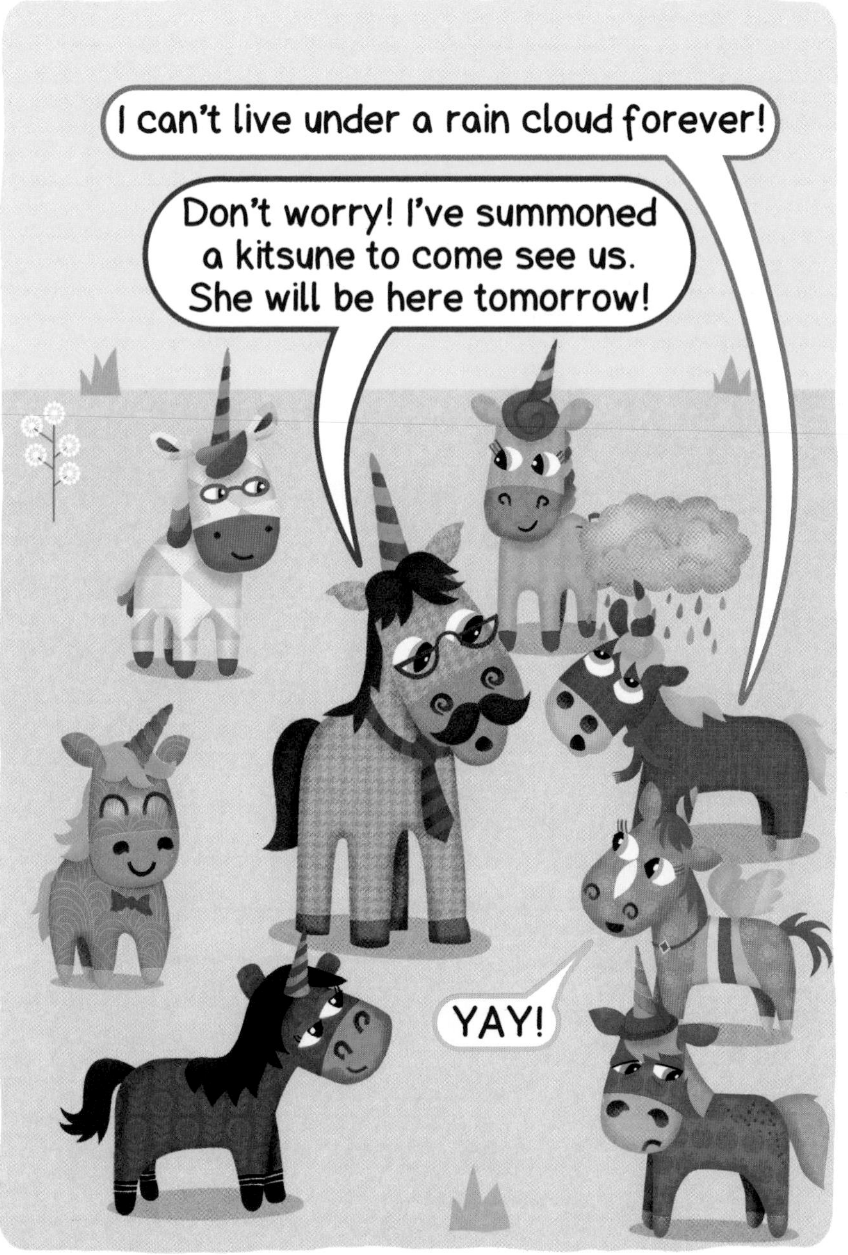
I can't live under a rain cloud forever!
Don't worry! I've summoned a kitsune to come see us. She will be here tomorrow!
YAY!

At **CLOUDTIME**, everyone was super excited about meeting the kitsune.

I noticed that Sunny looked a bit worried, so I asked what was the matter.

I've never been sick before, so I'm just a bit nervous.

Oh, don't worry, Sunny. I saw a kitsune before, when I had Fairy Pox. They were super gentle and kind. And they can have up to <u>nine</u> tails!

Wow, that is cool.

ACHOO!

I'll go get the broom.

4

Dr. Cloudberry

We were all eating breakfast when I noticed something shiny flying toward us.

Suddenly, the star flashed and a kitsune appeared in front of us!

Hello! I'm Dr. Cloudberry. Sorry about my surprising arrival, but stardust is the best way to travel.

Wow!

Wow!

Dr. Cloudberry was so lovely and friendly!

Before Mr. Rumptwinkle could continue, we all had a sneezing fit!

My goodness! This is the worst case of the Glitter Bug I have ever seen!

ACHOO!

ACHOO!

ACHOO!

ACHOO!

ACHOO!

ACHOO!

ACHOO!

But just look at all the pretty sparkles!

Then poor Monty sneezed and suddenly changed size! He hit his head on a tree branch.

Ouch.

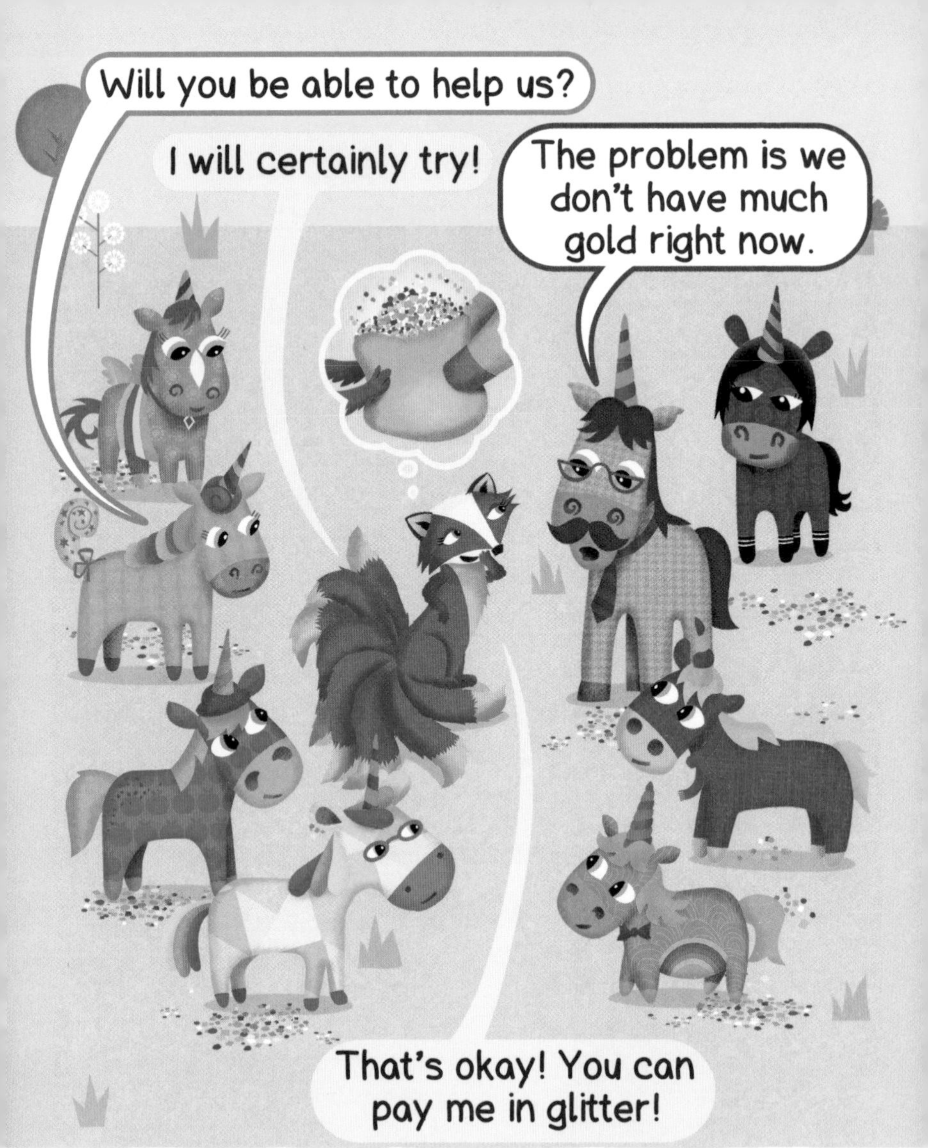
Will you be able to help us?
I will certainly try!
The problem is we don't have much gold right now.
That's okay! You can pay me in glitter!

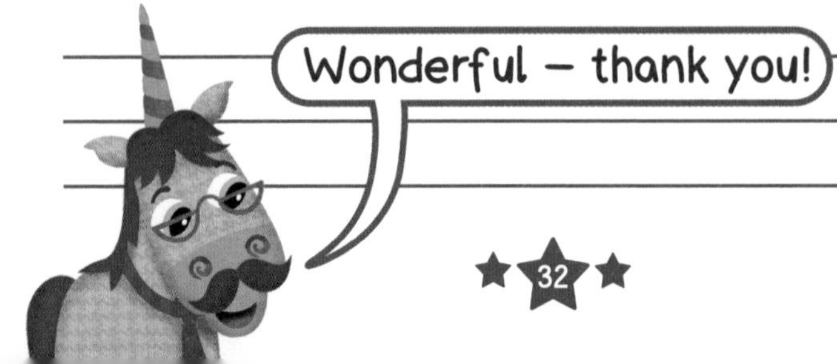
Wonderful – thank you!

Dr. Cloudberry
decided to examine
each of us one by one
in the **UNIPOD**. She
asked Piper to help
her, and Piper was
over the moon!

I could tell that Sunny was still feeling a bit worried about seeing the doctor.

Dr. Cloudberry was happy to examine me and Sunny at the same time. I think she noticed that Sunny was feeling worried, so she told him a joke!

This made both of us giggle and
actually helped us to stop sneezing a bit.

First, Dr. Cloudberry and Piper took our temperatures.

Next, they felt our pulses.

And then they examined our bellies,
which made us giggle.

Sorry if that tickles. Almost done!

Before we left, Dr. Cloudberry asked if we had any questions.

I was wondering about your lovely tails. You have eight, right?

I do! And one day I hope to have nine! Kitsunes get more tails for doing kind and clever things.

Eight is already quite a lot!

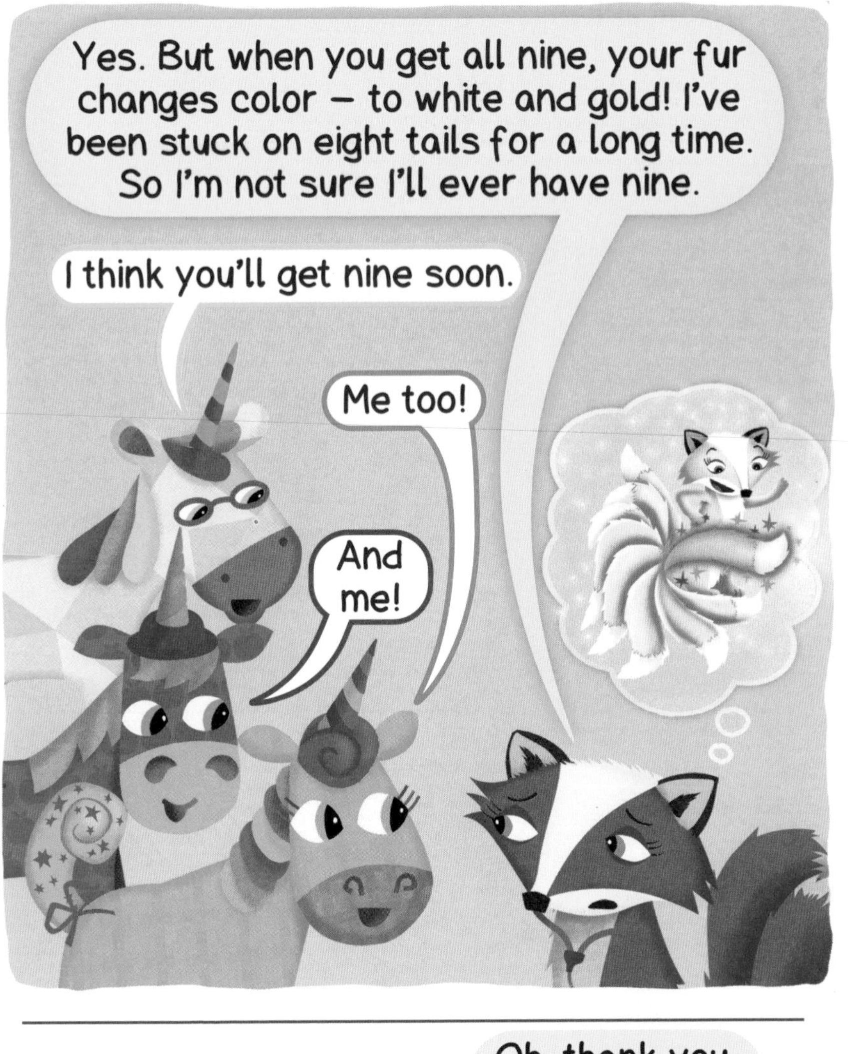
Yes. But when you get all nine, your fur changes color – to white and gold! I've been stuck on eight tails for a long time. So I'm not sure I'll ever have nine.
I think you'll get nine soon.
Me too!
And me!

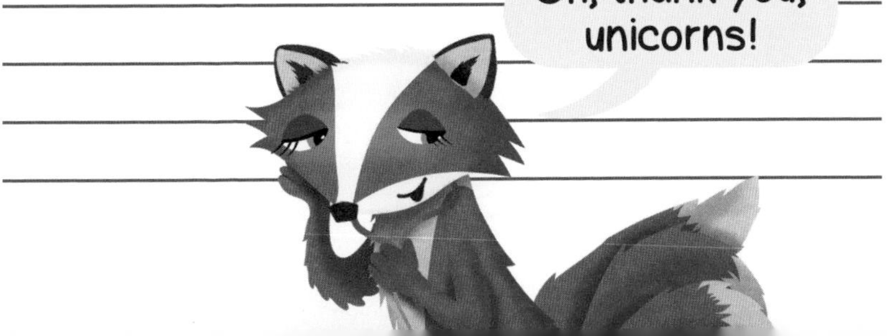
Oh, thank you, unicorns!

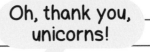

When we left the doctor, Sunny and I were feeling pretty good.

It's great that we're both feeling better already!

Maybe we don't have the bug anymore?!

Then we both sneezed.

ACHOO!

ACHOO!

Oh.

At **CLOUDTIME**, we were still sneezing.
But we were happy to have seen the doctor.

Diary, what if we never stop sneezing?

Thursday

This morning we were all still sneezing when Dr. Cloudberry arrived. We were feeling a bit down, but then she told a joke!

Good morning, unicorns! Quick question: What do you wear on your feet that sounds like a sneeze? . . . A-SHOE!

HA HA!

HA HA!

HA HA!

HA HA!

HA HA!

The joke was so silly, but we all started laughing! AND we all stopped sneezing!

Hmmm, that confirms it!

What is it, Dr. Cloudberry? Do you know how to make us better?

Yes, Sunny. I believe I do!

We all gathered around, excited to hear how Dr. Cloudberry would cure us.

Well, unicorns. After all my tests with my assistant Piper, I now know exactly what will make the Glitter Bug go away!

Do we need to take medicine?

Yes, a teaspoon.

Okay, but will we need anything else with the medicine?

Well, there is a special trick that will make you feel better faster.

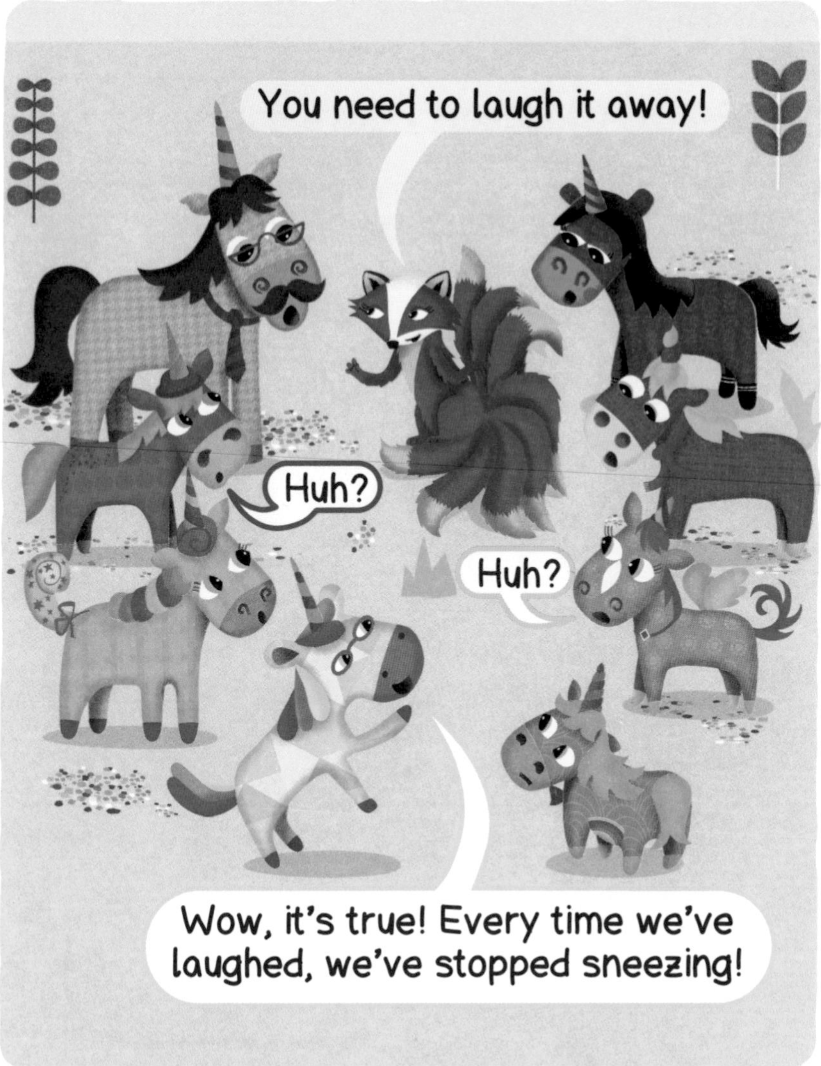
You need to laugh it away!
Huh?
Huh?
Wow, it's true! Every time we've laughed, we've stopped sneezing!

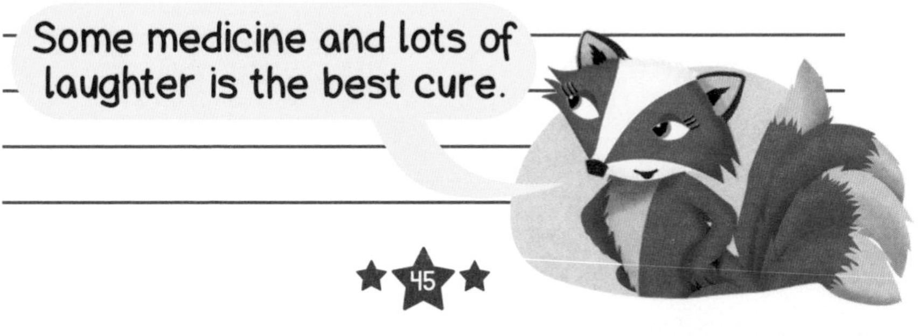
Some medicine and lots of laughter is the best cure.

So Dr. Cloudberry gave each of us a teaspoon of medicine. But having the Glitter Bug meant none of us really felt like laughing.

It's difficult to laugh when random things keep popping out of my mane.

Yeah. I keep making it rain or blowing a tornado.

And I keep changing size and hitting my head.

And I keep losing Sunny when he suddenly goes invisible.

How are we supposed to laugh when we keep sneezing and getting interrupted by our powers?

Unicorns, you can do this. I have seen that you are all great at being positive even when bad stuff is happening.

Dr. Cloudberry is right, unicorns! Let's plan a comedy show that you can perform tomorrow!

A show? That does sound like fun!

YAY!

47

So we spent the rest of the day planning a comedy show.

Sunny and I started writing jokes.

Piper and Jed practiced a funny magic trick.

Monty, Scarlett, and Nutmeg worked on a clown act with unicycles and juggling.

By **CLOUDTIME**, we were very tired.

Oh, Diary. Trying to be funny when you feel sick sure is tough, and also very tirin –

6

Clowning Around

As we practiced for the comedy show, we started losing hope that we could make one another laugh!

Our act just keeps going wrong!

I know! Every time I try not to sneeze, I end up —

ACHOO!

We put some tables out to build a stage.

Do you think this show is going to work?

All we can do is try our hardest to make one another laugh.

ACHOO!

Finally, it was showtime!

Other magical creatures turned up to watch our comedy show!

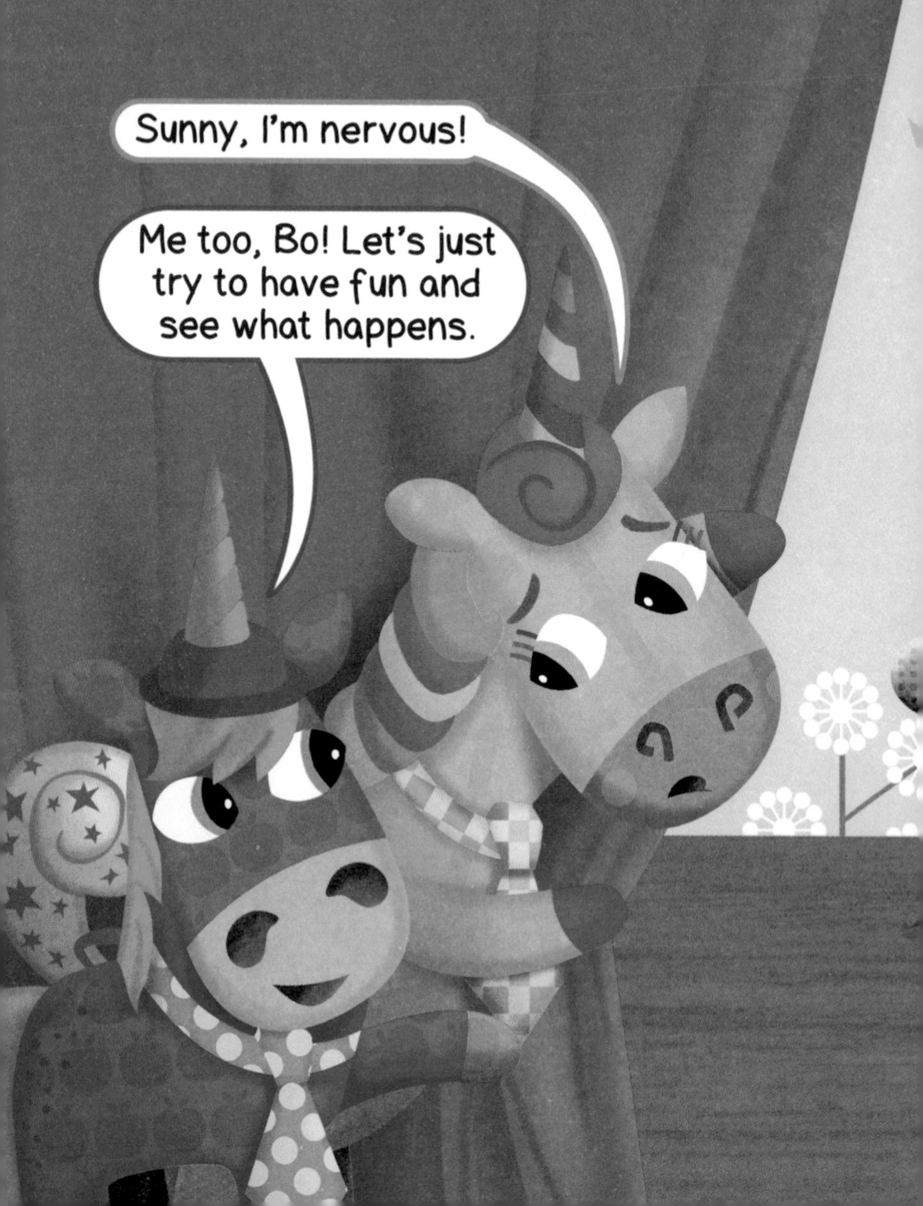

Feeling a bit shaky on our hooves,
Sunny and I went out onstage . . .

Good evening, everyone! Welcome to the Unicorns' Comedy Show!
I'm Sunny and this is my comedy partner B–ACHOO!
Well, actually, it's not Bachoo. My name is Bo!
And if you're wondering what Bo is short for . . .
Um, I'm not that short!
No. I meant your name, silly!

Oh dear, Diary. We were sneezing so much that all our jokes came out wrong!

Next onstage were Piper and Jed.
Their magic show also went a bit wrong!

For our first trick, we will magic
a rabbit out of this hat!

Abracadabr —

ACHOO!

Jed's sneeze made his power go off,
and it started to snow onstage!

Um, the rabbit doesn't like the
cold, so she won't come out!

Come on out, little bunny rab —

ACHOO!

When Piper sneezed, Jed AND the rabbit ended up covered in bandages!

Finally, Monty, Scarlett, and Nutmeg went onstage to do their clown act. Well. They <u>tried</u> to do it.

Then all three of them sneezed.

ACHOO!

ACHOO!

HA! HA! HA! HA! HA! HA! HA!

I felt so bad that nothing was going right.

Monty, Scarlett, and Nutmeg ran offstage to join the rest of us unicorns.

Then I looked out at the audience. And I realized something.

Everyone looked at the audience, which was rolling around laughing! Then we all looked at one another.

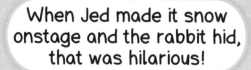

We burst out laughing, too.

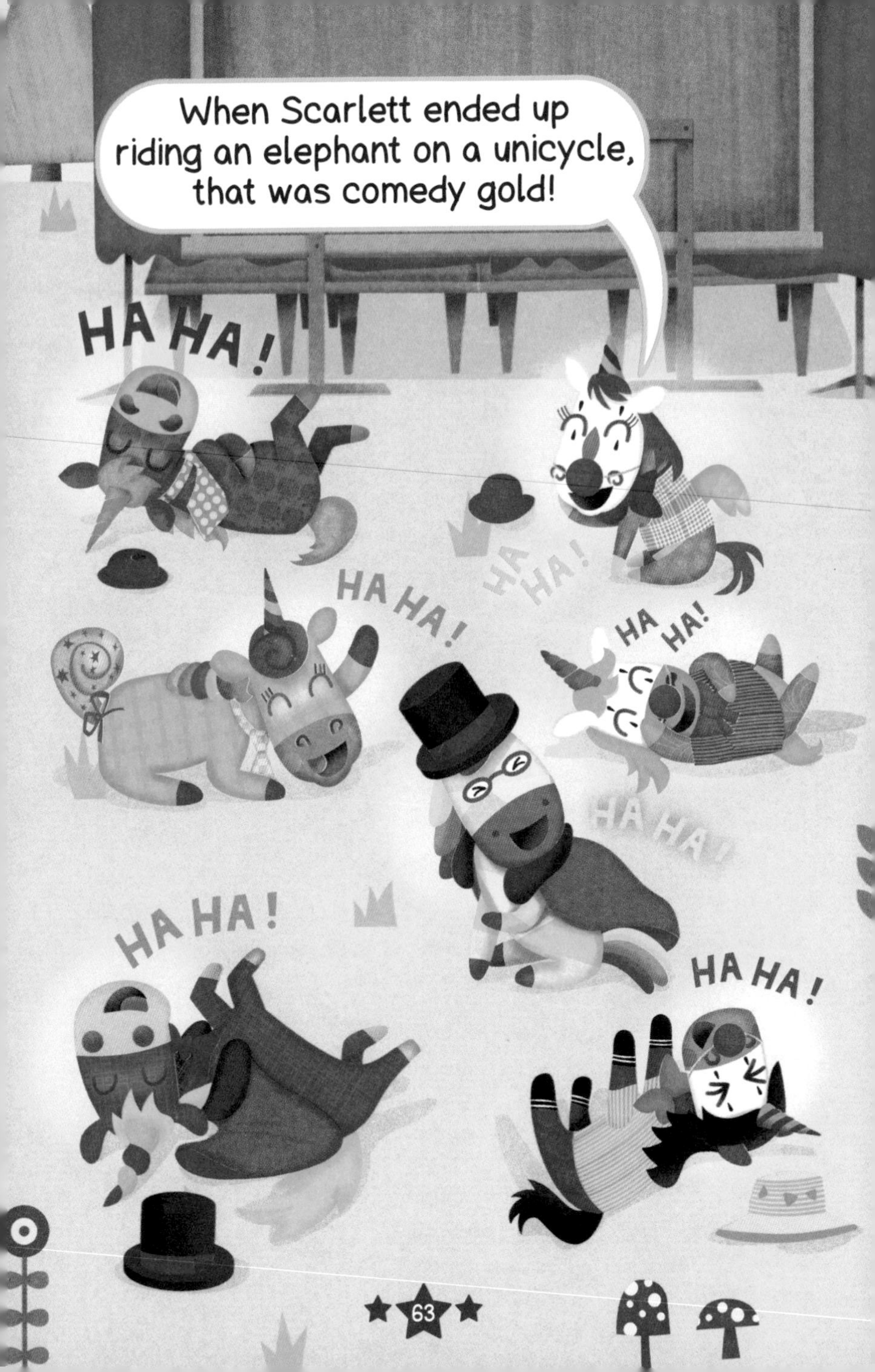
When Scarlett ended up riding an elephant on a unicycle, that was comedy gold!
HA HA!
HA HA!
HA HA!
HA HA!
HA HA!
HA HA!
HA HA!

Mr. Rumptwinkle and Dr. Cloudberry joined us backstage.

We went out onstage and took a bow.

Then Mr. Rumptwinkle made an announcement.

Unicorns, I am so proud that you managed to make one another — and all of us — laugh! So you <u>have</u> earned a new patch!

We were given a LAUGHTER PATCH!

What a day, Diary! I really hope
Dr. Cloudberry gets her ninth tail after
fixing our bug!

7

The Golden Kitsune

Saturday

We slept so well last night — without any sneezing! But Piper looked sad, so I asked her what was wrong.

Now that we're better, Dr. Cloudberry will leave.

I know you liked being her helper, Piper. We'll all miss her.

Dr. Cloudberry ate breakfast with us before she left.

Thank you for curing us, Dr. Cloudberry!

Well, really you made yourselves better by being so funny and taking medicine, too. And thank you for all the glitter!

I guess you're —

ACHOO!

Oh no! You can't still be sick?!

With all her glitter, Dr. Cloudberry did one more thing for us before she left . . .

She used the glitter to face-paint all of us. We looked **GLITTERRIFIC**!

Suddenly, sparkles appeared around Dr. Cloudberry. She grew a ninth tail! And her fur changed color, too — to white and gold!

Oh wow!

Painting our faces must have been the extra kind thing that earned you your last tail!

After Dr. Cloudberry left, we all sat down for a sneeze-free dinner together.

Sunny got **CLOUD PIE** all over his face!

It's true, Diary: Laughter really is the best medicine!

Rebecca Elliott may not have a magical horn or sneeze glitter, but she's still a lot like a unicorn. Rebecca always tries to have a positive attitude, she likes to laugh a lot, and she lives with some great creatures — her noisy-yet-charming children, her lovable but naughty dog, Frida, and a big, lazy cat named Bernard. She gets to hang out with these fun characters and write stories for a living, so she thinks her life is pretty magical!

Rebecca is the author of several picture books, the young adult novel PRETTY FUNNY FOR A GIRL, the bestselling Unicorn Diaries early chapter book series, and the bestselling Owl Diaries series.

Unicorn Diaries

How much do you know about The Glitter Bug?

In Japanese folklore, kitsunes are foxes with special powers. Reread Chapter 1. What are four fun facts about kitsunes?

Reread Chapter 2. What is the Glitter Bug? How does sneezing affect each unicorn's powers?

Dr. Cloudberry comes to examine the sick unicorns. According to the doctor, what is the cure for the Glitter Bug?

The unicorns put on a comedy show. How does each unicorn prepare? Why are Bo and Sunny nervous to go onstage on page 53?

How do the unicorns pay Dr. Cloudberry for her help? What happens to Dr. Cloudberry's fur when she earns her ninth tail?